THIS BOOK IS TO BE RETURNED ON OR BEFORE THE
LAST DATE STAMPED BELOW

Balfron 01360 440407   Bannockburn 01786 812286   Bridge of Allan 01786 833680
Callander 01877 331544   Cambusbarron 01786 473873   Central 01786 237760
Cowie 01786 816269   Doune 01786 841732   Drymen 01360 660751
Dunblane 01786 823125   Fallin 01786 812492   Killin 01567 820571
Plean 01786 816319   St Ninians 01786 472069   Strathblane 01360 770737
                          Library HQ 01786 237535

STIRLING COUNCIL LIBRARIES

7441

Tilda Kelly

Special thanks to Linda Chapman.
Illustrations by Gavin Scott and The Bright Agency.

With thanks to Inclusive Minds for connecting us with their Inclusion Ambassador network, in particular Anna Brown for her input.

ORCHARD BOOKS

First published in Great Britain in 2020 by The Watts Publishing Group

1 3 5 7 9 10 8 6 4 2

A CIP catalogue record for this book
is available from the British Library.

ISBN 978 1 40836 334 8

Printed and bound in Great Britain by Clays Ltd, Elcograf S.p.A
The paper and board used in this book are made from wood from responsible sources.

Orchard Books
An imprint of
Hachette Children's Group
Part of The Watts Publishing Group Limited
Carmelite House
50 Victoria Embankment
London EC4Y 0DZ

An Hachette UK Company
www.hachette.co.uk
www.hachettechildrens.co.uk

Contents

Chapter One

Ruby Turner turned the pages of her animal encyclopaedia. As her eyes ran over the pages on marsupials, she recited the facts in her head. *Red kangaroo weight: 150kg; hairy-nosed wombat weight: 40kg . . .*

When Ruby was older, she was going to be a vet and work at Green Gates

Wildlife Sanctuary where her mum had a job as a nurse. She pushed her chin-length, brown hair behind her ears and continued with her list:

koala: 15kg; Tasmanian devil: 14kg . . .

"Ruby, it's time to go home now." Mrs Hanson, Ruby's teacher, came over to her desk.

Wallaby: 5.5kg; bush-tail possum: 4.5kg; potoroo; 1.7kg . . . Ruby finished in a rush and jumped to her feet, worried that Mrs Hanson might put a hand on her arm.

When people touched her it made her skin feel prickly.

"Did you know there are 235 species of marsupial in Australia? And 334 species in the world?" she asked her teacher.

"No, I didn't," said Mrs Hanson, smiling. "It's clear in the corridor now." She nodded towards where the last few girls were leaving, arms linked, faces close as they chattered about what they were going to do when the summer holidays started. Ruby hated going into the corridor at the end of the school day. She didn't like the way the other kids all talked really loudly and jostled each other as they got their school bags. Mrs

Hanson understood and let her sit and read until everyone had gone.

"Remember to pick up your painting on the way out," Mrs Hanson said. "See you on Monday, Ruby."

Ruby frowned. Her mum had explained that "see you" was just a way of saying goodbye, but it always seemed a weird thing to say. Of course Mrs Hanson would see her on Monday. Why did she feel she had to say it? But she remembered to be polite. "Goodbye," she said and she walked to the corridor.

Through the open door, she could see her mum, wearing shorts and a long floaty top, her dark, wavy hair just touching her shoulders. Ruby collected her painting from where it was drying on the rack and went out into the sunshine, feeling a rush of relief. It was always good to get out of school. She didn't like being surrounded by other kids and having to do what everyone else was doing even when she didn't want to do it. And there were so many rules to remember – not to interrupt people when they were speaking; not to stand too close to people; to say *please* and *thank you* and *sorry*.

"Another new picture?" said Mum, as Ruby reached her. "Hmm . . . let me guess. Is it Cooper?"

"Yes!" said Ruby, beaming, as she showed her the picture. She loved to draw Cooper. He was her dog – a golden retriever with a coat the colour of damp sand, a wagging, feathery tail and melting chocolate-brown eyes.

"Oh, Ruby, it's excellent! It's so like him!" her mum said, taking it. "He looks

just like that when he wants you to throw his ball for him."

Ruby felt a flush of pride. She'd spent ages on the picture, carefully sketching the outline in pencil first and then using watercolours and a fine brush to add shading and colour. When she wasn't reading, she loved to paint. Her pictures were always very neat and carefully done with fine lines and watercolours. She didn't like thick, sticky oil paint. The feel of it on her skin made her shiver all over.

"We'll have to put it on the wall," her mum said. One wall in their kitchen was covered in a massive pinboard where

Mum and Dad pinned Ruby's best pictures.

"Let's go and put it up now," said Ruby eagerly.

"Soon. We're actually not going home straight away," said Mum.

Ruby frowned. It was Friday, and on Fridays, she and Mum always went straight home and had a snack of apple slices that they dipped in smooth peanut butter. After their snack, Ruby sat at the table and drew while Mum cooked chicken fingers, peas and mashed potato. Dad would come home at six o'clock and they would all sit down to eat together. That was how Fridays worked.

Ruby didn't like things to change. Her voice rose as an anxious knot tightened inside her. "Why aren't we going home?" she demanded. "Why?"

"Don't worry, Ruby," Mum said, in the soothing voice she used when Ruby got stressed over things. "There's no need to be upset. We're not going straight home because we have to call in at Green Gates. That's OK, isn't it?"

Ruby felt the knot inside her loosen. Next to home, Green Gates Wildlife Sanctuary was her favourite place in the whole world, so going there, although it wasn't what they usually did on Friday, was more than OK.

"I had an appointment this afternoon and I have to pick up some paperwork for the weekend," said Mum. "Carl has just finished the extension to the koala kindergarten. The young koalas are loving it. I thought you'd like to see them."

A wide smile split Ruby's face. "I want to go there now!" she said and, not waiting for her mum, she set off at a run across the playground.

Chapter Two

On the drive to the sanctuary, Mum asked Ruby how school had been. "We had a maths test," Ruby told her. "It was the best bit of the day." She knew the other girls on her table thought she was weird, but one of her favourite things at school was maths tests. She liked the clean, white test sheet with spaces for the answers. She liked that everyone had to be quiet during tests and she nearly always got all of the questions right.

"What else did you do?" Mum asked.

"We had to write a story." Ruby pulled a face. Writing stories was one of her least favourite things. Mrs Hanson liked to bring in an object and put it on the table – it might be a key, a piece of rope, or a delicate jewelled box – and everyone had to write a story about the object. Ruby's stories were usually very short and always had lots of facts in them. She liked facts. They were comforting and real.

"Look, it's your new school," Mum said as they drove past Arthur Phillip High, a large high school with low brick buildings and playing fields round the back. Ruby stared at the car ceiling, not wanting to look. She really didn't want to start at high school after the summer holidays. She'd been in for a visit day a few weeks ago with the rest of her class and she hadn't liked it. It was noisy, the lights were bright and she hadn't liked the smells in the canteen.

"I think you'll enjoy it there," Mum said. "You'll be able to join the Art Club and Maths Club. It will be a chance to make new friends."

Ruby wondered whether to tell Mum
that you couldn't have new friends if
you didn't have old friends. There were
the girls who shared her table in class
but they weren't friends. They went
round in a group together and had
sleepovers and parties that she wasn't
invited to. Sometimes it made her feel
lonely but most of the time she just felt
curious. What would it be like to have a
friend? Not a dog friend like Cooper but
a human friend.

They arrived at the sanctuary, which
had two wide green gates with a wooden
sign that arched over the driveway. It
had the words Green Gates Wildlife

Sanctuary painted on it. There was a cluster of single-story white buildings and a car park in front. Ruby followed her mum through the automatic doors that slid open as they approached. She breathed in the clean smell of disinfectant as they crossed the tidy reception area with its green floor.

Jean, the receptionist, greeted her. "Hey, Ruby. How are you doing?"

"I'm happy," Ruby told her. "I'm going to see the koalas." She noticed something. "Your hair looks different."

Jean's red hair usually reached past her shoulders but it had been cut so now it stopped at her chin. "Yes," she said. "I had it cut yesterday."

"I don't like it," Ruby said.

"Ruby!" her mum said. Ruby often told the truth without thinking.

"It's OK, Lisa," said Jean, giving Mum an understanding look.

"It looks good but I don't like it because it's different," Ruby explained to Jean.

"Sorry!" Mum mouthed as Jean buzzed them through to the back.

"No worries," said Jean good-naturedly. "How was your hospital appointment?"

"Good. I'll tell you about it later," said Mum, as she and Ruby went through to the back of the sanctuary.

"Hospital appointment?" Ruby asked her. "Why did you go to the hospital? Are you sick?"

"No, it was just a check-up, nothing to worry about," said Mum.

A check-up was fine. Ruby stopped worrying and hurried ahead. The corridors behind reception led to an operating theatre and an examination room where the vets checked over any animals who were brought in. There were storerooms with medical and food supplies, a staff room and, best of all, the animal nurseries where the baby animals were looked after. Outside, through another set of doors were the animal enclosures where older animals were kept until they were ready to be released back into the wild.

There were people bustling around – nurses in their green overalls, vets in their blue ones and the volunteers in their jeans or shorts and sturdy boots. They passed the wallaby nursery where orphaned joeys – baby wallabies – were kept in fleece slings that mimicked their mother's pouches. Looking in through the glass door, Ruby saw Tara, the centre manager, sitting on a bench, feeding a tiny joey. It was wrapped in a blue blanket and she was dropping milk from a pipette into its mouth, one drop at a time.

"Mum! Look!" breathed Ruby, stopping.

"I know," said Mum. "He's only about three months old."

"Can we go in?" Ruby asked eagerly.

"Yes. But wash your hands first," Mum reminded her, heading over to a sink outside the room where there was antibacterial soap and an air dryer. Ruby joined her. Baby animals could pick up infections really easily so it was very important to wash your hands before coming into contact with them. They also covered their shoes with plastic shoe liners to avoid bringing in any germs from outside.

As they opened the door, Tara smiled. "Come to see Bertie?" she said, nodding at the tiny joey.

"Yes, he's beautiful," said Ruby, looking at the tiny joey's screwed-up eyes and pointed snout, his muzzle coated with milk. "Where's his mum?"

"He was found near the creek with her," said Tara. "She died but he survived. Do you want to hold him?"

"Yes!" Ruby whispered, knowing she mustn't shout or make a loud noise in case it startled the baby animal.

She sat down and Tara handed Bertie

over. Ruby held the joey, wrapped up
in his cocoon of blankets, and carefully
guided the drops of milk into his mouth.
He snuggled closer. "You're a natural
at this, Ruby," said Tara with a smile.
"You'll be taking over my job soon."

"I'd like that," said Ruby, feeling a

wave of happiness as she gazed down at the little joey's sweet face. She found people hard to understand but animals were easy. They needed food and water, to be kept warm and safe, and then they were content. People wanted more than that.

When Bertie fell asleep and Tara took him back to tuck him up in his pouch, Ruby and her mum headed on to the koala kindergarten. Ruby loved the koalas with their plump, heavy bodies, their soft fur, their little dark eyes and big tufted ears. They moved slowly and didn't make loud noises. Baby koalas were called joeys, like baby wallabies.

The babies were looked after in the koala nursery but when they got older – at about a year – they were moved to the koala kindergarten. It was an enclosure outside with eucalyptus trees for them to feed from, climb and sleep in. It helped them get used to living like adult koalas. Then, when they were about eighteen months old, they were released back into the wild.

Over the last few months, there had been quite a few bushfires and the number of koalas in the sanctuary had risen. Carl, one of the volunteers who came in to help out, had been extending the koala kindergarten. He had planted more eucalyptus trees and added a bigger climbing frame made from branches. There were baskets hanging from the branches for the young koalas to rest in.

As she and Mum went through the door that led from the air-conditioned rooms to the outside world, Ruby breathed in the strong animal smell. It was strange – she didn't like some strong smells, but she never minded the scent of animals. Carl was standing outside the wire meshing of the koala kindergarten.

"Hey, Rubes!" he said, holding up his hand for a high five. Ruby hit it with her own then quickly pulled her hand away.

"Is it finished?" she asked eagerly, wiping her hand on her shorts. She'd been to visit several times over the last few weeks while Carl had been hard at work.

"You bet it is! Look at how the little fellas are enjoying it."

"It looks great, Carl," said Mum. "They definitely needed more space. We were running out of room fast."

Ruby stared into the enclosure. There were about fifteen koalas climbing the trees, their dark claws gripping the branches. Others were resting in the forks of the trees, their eyes half closed, and two were peering out of the wicker

baskets hanging in the branches.

A grey koala edged along a branch near to the wire mesh and peered down curiously at them.

"Can I go in?" Ruby asked longingly.

But her mum shook her head. "The less contact these koalas have with humans the better. If they get too used to humans they'll be in danger when they're released. We don't want that."

Ruby felt frustrated that she couldn't hold the koalas but she tried to fight the feeling because what Mum said made sense. The koalas needed to be safe.

"Maybe you could draw them instead," Mum suggested.

Ruby liked that idea. She took her sketch pad out of her school bag and plonked herself down on the ground. Then she set to work, while her mum and Carl chatted.

"Tara was telling me the koala nursery is just about full to the brim," said Carl.

"It is. I don't know what we'll do if we get any more orphans coming in," said Mum. "We can barely cope as it is."

"The bushfires have a lot to answer for," said Carl. "So many koalas lost their homes and got injured. We've had a lot of people bringing them in these last few weeks."

"Let's hope the fires are under control now," said Mum.

Ruby stopped listening as she bent over her drawing, her pencil making quick lines on the paper as she sketched the koala who was staring down at her. Bear-like nose, curious eyes, fluffy ears . . . Ruby sighed happily as she lost herself in drawing and let the rest of the confusing world fade away.

Chapter Three

"Cucumber done. Carrots done. Celery next!" announced Ruby. It was a week after her visit to the sanctuary and her summer holidays had started. She was helping her dad in the kitchen by chopping up vegetables. Monday was spaghetti bolognaise and salad night.

Cooper, who was sitting watching Ruby, whined. She fed him a piece of carrot and his tail thumped on the floor. Ruby bent down and hugged him. "I love you," she told him as he snuffled her hair.

"Careful, I might get jealous!" said Dad with a smile as he stirred a tin of tomatoes into the meat in the frying pan. He was a Maths teacher, which meant he was able to look after Ruby in the school holidays. He glanced at the clock. "Mum should be home soon. She rang earlier and said they were having a really busy day. More fires have started."

Ruby remembered the conversation her mum and Carl had been having when she'd been at the sanctuary. "I hope there's enough space for all the animals who are brought in."

She fetched the celery and began to chop it into neat slices and then she arranged little piles of celery, carrot and cucumber on to her dinner plate. She didn't like it when a salad was mixed up. Dad took the chopping board with the remaining salad ingredients on and tossed them all into a big bowl with some salad dressing for him and Mum.

There was the sound of the front door opening and Mum came in. She looked hot, her hair sticking to her damp forehead. "What a day," she said, sinking down into a chair.

"You look exhausted," said Dad. "Are you OK?"

"Mum! Mum! I found a new animal website today. It had loads of interesting facts. Did you know 80 per cent of koala habitat has been lost around the world because of humans?" Ruby said. "And—"

"Ruby, honey, just give Mum a few minutes," said Dad. "Can you get her a glass of water?"

Ruby frowned. She wanted to tell Mum all about the things she had found out. She didn't want to wait.

"Ruby," said Dad, fixing her with a look.

Ruby huffed and went to get the water.

"Are you really OK?" Dad said quietly to Mum.

"I'm fine," said Mum. "It's just been a full-on day and I've hardly sat down. We've had wallabies, wombats and koalas all coming in because of the fires."

"Well, you relax now," said Dad, dropping a kiss on her head. "Ruby and I will get dinner sorted."

Soon, they were sitting down to eat. Ruby just had plain pasta with grated cheese instead of bolognaise sauce. She didn't like food that had lots of ingredients jumbled up together. She didn't know how Mum and Dad could bear to eat salad with all the ingredients mixed up and then coated with slimy dressing. Yuck!

As Mum helped herself to some more spaghetti from the pot on the table, Ruby frowned. "You shouldn't eat any more," she said, looking at the way her mum's shorts were stretching over her tummy. "You're getting fat."

"Ruby," said Dad. "We don't say things

like that to people, remember?"

"But it's true," Ruby protested.

"Maybe it is," said Mum, glancing down at her tummy. "But Dad's right, some people might get upset if you point out they're putting on weight, Ruby."

"I wouldn't mind if people told me," said Ruby with a shrug. "Not if it was true."

"I know, possum," said Dad. "But other people are different to you and they *will* mind, so best not to do it, OK?"

"OK," sighed Ruby.

"So, what have you two been doing today?" said Mum, tucking into her spaghetti. "Did you go get some

Christmas presents like you planned?"

Ruby shook her head. Dad had wanted to go but she'd refused to leave the house. She hated the shopping centre.

"Ruby wasn't feeling it today," said Dad, exchanging looks with Mum. "But maybe tomorrow, hey?"

Ruby felt her stomach start to tie itself in knots. She really didn't want to go to the shopping centre. She started to shake her head but just then the phone rang and Dad went to answer it.

"We can always leave Christmas shopping a little while longer," said Mum softly. "Don't get upset, sweetie."

Ruby concentrated on counting the

vegetables left on her plate. Counting was good; it helped her calm down.

Dad came back in, frowning. "That was the chief of the Rural Fire Service. Another bushfire's broken out. They need help. I'd better get out there."

Mum and Dad were both firies – volunteer firefighters with the RFS. It was how they had met.

Dad started to pull on his boots.

"But it's Mum's turn to go, not yours, Dad," said Ruby. Her parents normally took it in turns when the fire service needed help. "You went last time."

"I'm not going out tonight, Ruby," said Mum. "Dad will go instead."

Ruby frowned. "But what about me? Dad and I always watch *Wildlife Wonders* together on Mondays."

"You can watch it with Mum instead," said Dad. He gently held her arms, his eyes on hers. "I'm sorry, Ruby. I really am. But I have to go. People – and animals – are depending on me." He went to the door. "Goodbye. I'll be here in the morning when you wake up, I promise."

Ruby could hear her breathing get louder and feel her tummy tightening. She knew her dad had to go but she didn't want him to. She wanted him to stay and sit with her and watch

Wildlife Wonders like they always did on Mondays. She pushed her chair back with an abrupt scraping sound.

"Ruby?" her mum said. "Do you want to talk?"

"No!" Ruby cried. She ran to her bedroom and threw herself down on her bed. Tears sprang to her eyes.

Hearing a slight creak, she looked round. Cooper's black nose appeared around her bedroom door and then his muzzle, his head and his whole body. He trotted over to her and put his head on the bed beside her and whined softly. Slipping off the bed, Ruby sat on the floor and put her arms round him. She

buried her face in the thick fur around
his neck and he gently licked her arms.

"I don't feel right," she whispered to
Cooper. "I feel all twisty inside." She
pulled back and looked into his soft
brown eyes. Warmth filled her and she
felt her frustration fade. He always
looked at her in the same way. He

never thought she was rude or weird or difficult. He loved her, no matter what.

"Ruby?" She looked up. Her mum was standing in the doorway. "I'm sorry you're upset and that Dad had to go out," she said softly. She held open her arms. Ruby hesitated but then went over and leant against her. Mum's arms folded around her. Ruby didn't hug her back; she didn't like hugging people, only animals. But as she breathed in Mum's familiar scent – a trace of coconut shampoo, a hint of the sanctuary's hand disinfectant – she felt better. Cooper joined them, nudging his nose between them, wanting to share the hug.

Ruby smiled and stroked him.

"How about we all go and watch *Wildlife Wonders* together?" Mum said.

Ruby nodded and they went downstairs.

Ruby stayed awake that night until Dad came in, his face blackened with soot, his eyes red from the heat of the fires. Only then, knowing he was safe, did she let herself fall asleep. The sound of Cooper barking in the yard woke her in the early morning. It wasn't a loud bark, more just a yip. She heard it again and frowned. Why was he barking? He didn't usually bark at this time of the morning.

Getting out of bed, she padded to the window and looked out. The sun was just starting to rise, its pale rays streaking across the dawn sky. The sky was the lightest blue, the gum trees at the end of the grass were a dark green. Everywhere looked clean and fresh. Ruby's eyes searched for Cooper. There he was, curled up on the decking near the back door. He liked to sleep outside when it was really hot in the summer. He lifted his head and made the strange yipping sound again, almost like he wanted to bark but was trying not to make too much noise. Weird.

Ruby decided to go and check he was OK. She hurried downstairs then let herself out of the back door. "Cooper?" she called softly.

Cooper pricked his ears and whined but didn't get up as she hurried to him.

"Cooper? Are you OK— Oh!" Ruby broke off with a gasp, stopping dead in her tracks. "Koala!" she whispered in shock. Nestled between Cooper's front paws was a sleeping baby koala!

Chapter Four

"Well, well, well," said Mum, shaking her head as she carefully carried the baby koala into the kitchen. The joey clung to her arms, looking round in confusion with his small dark eyes.

"Where did he come from, Mum?" Ruby demanded.

"I have no idea," said Mum. "It's really unusual for koalas to come this close to where people live. The only thing I can think of is that he must have fallen off his mum's back, crawled into our yard from the bush reserve down the road and snuggled up to Cooper for warmth."

"What are we going to do with him?" said Ruby.

"He's only about nine months old by the look of it," Mum said, stroking the joey's fur. "Too young to survive without his mother. Dad's out checking to see if he can find the mum but if he can't we're going to have to take him into the sanctuary. First though, we need to get him some water."

Ruby hurried to the tap.

"No, get water from the kettle," said Mum. "It boiled earlier so it should have cooled down now. And I need a medicine dispenser – one of the ones I used to use if I had to give you liquid paracetamol when you were little. But wash your hands first."

Ruby did as she was asked and brought the things over. Mum filled the plastic medicine dispenser with the cooled boiled water and let the koala joey have some, drop by drop.

Dad came in, shaking his head. "There's no sign of a mother koala."

"We need to get him checked over by a vet," said Mum. "Then we can settle him into the nursery there and try and find him a foster mum."

"If there's space," said Ruby, remembering the conversation from the day before.

Mum looked worried. "Yes, if there's space."

Ruby stroked the soft grey fur on the top of the koala's head. He looked at her with scared dark eyes. "Don't worry, little Pablo," she said softly. "We'll help you."

"Pablo?" questioned Mum.

"After Pablo Picasso," said Ruby. He was one of her favourite artists. "Born in

1881 and died in 1973. He lived in—"

"OK, you can tell me more on the way
to the sanctuary," Mum broke in.

They wrapped Pablo in a clean towel
and Mum let Ruby hold him as she
drove. He clung to her arm with his

sharp black claws and Ruby could feel his heart beating fast. She knew he must be wondering where he was and what was happening.

"You're going to be OK," she told him softly. "We'll find you a foster mum at the sanctuary and then you can stay there until you're old enough to leave. I'll come and visit you lots."

He cuddled closer into her arms.

When they got to the sanctuary, Mum told Ruby to wait outside the examining room while she took Pablo to be checked over. Ruby didn't like waiting. She paced up and down impatiently.

"Well?" she said as Mum and Tara came over with Pablo. He was asleep in Mum's arms, wrapped in a blue fleece blanket.

"The vet said Pablo's quite healthy," said Mum. "But there isn't any room in the nursery for him to stay here."

"We're going to ring round and try and find another sanctuary to take him," said Tara.

Ruby held out her arms. Mum handed Pablo to her. He was snuggled into the blanket, his eyes shut, his breathing soft and regular. He gave a little sigh as Ruby held him close to her chest. She felt a desperate urge to protect him. "No," she said, looking up abruptly at her mum. "He's not going." They were not taking Pablo far away from her.

"Oh, Ruby, sweetheart, I'm sorry but there just isn't room here," said Mum, sitting down beside her.

"And none of our local koala caretakers who look after orphaned joeys in their own homes have any spaces," said Tara. "I've already checked."

"I can be his caretaker," said Ruby, looking up at Tara. "You said I was a natural at looking after animals." The words tumbled out of her as the idea took hold in her mind. "I can look after

him and Mum can help. It's the summer
holidays, I'm home all the time and
when school starts again well, if there
isn't a space for him here, I can just miss
school and keep looking after him and—"

"Whoa, whoa!" said Mum, holding
her hands up. "Ruby, being a koala
caretaker is a huge commitment. You
have to bottle-feed a joey this age four
or five times a day as well as finding
them eucalyptus leaves to nibble on. And
because they're nocturnal animals, you
have to stay up in the night to feed them
and play with them. There is also no
way you're missing school, so you can
forget that idea right now."

"OK, I won't miss school but there are five weeks and three days of the summer holidays left," said Ruby. "I could look after Pablo and by the time school starts maybe there will be space here or one of the other caretakers will have room. I don't mind about it being a big commitment and you know all about koalas."

Tara looked at Mum. "You are qualified to be a koala carer, Lisa . . ."

"I don't know," said Mum, her eyes going to the sleeping joey in Ruby's arms. "Ruby, if we have him at home you'll get so attached to him you'll be really upset when he has to leave us to prepare for going back into the wild."

"I won't be because I know it's best for him," said Ruby simply. "Koalas aren't pets. I know that. But Pablo needs someone to look after him until he's a bit older. I can be that person. Please let me." She didn't think she had ever wanted anything as much as she wanted this in her entire life.

"You don't need to make a quick decision, Lisa," said Tara, seeing Mum hesitate. "You can think it over . . ."

"No," Mum decided. "We'll do it. We'll be his caretakers."

Ruby gasped. Pablo stirred in her arms and she wanted to jump and squeal and

dance around but she made herself stay still so she didn't scare him. "Thank you! Oh, thank you!" she whispered, cradling the little koala to her chest. Her eyes shone as she kissed him. "Pablo, you're coming home with me and I'm going to be the best koala caretaker ever! I'll do everything right. Just you wait and see!"

Chapter Five

"Let me show you how to make up the milk," Mum said, when they were back at home later. Pablo was sleeping in a round wicker basket that they had got from the centre. Ruby and Mum had lined it with fleecy blankets to keep him warm. Mum had also collected a crate of everything else they would need – bottles, teats, special milk powder, a steriliser to make sure there were no germs in the bottles and teats, a brush to clean the bottles and a supply of blankets because the ones in his basket would need washing every day.

Cooper sat and watched the basket on the table as if he was keeping guard over it. "Cooper's going to be a good caretaker too," said Ruby, stroking his head and floppy ears.

Mum showed her how to measure out the milk powder correctly into the bottles. "It's absolutely vital that you count exactly the right number of scoops

of powder and add the right amount
of water, otherwise his milk will be too
rich or too weak and it will make him
ill." Ruby nodded. She was good at
counting. Mum watched her as she made
up a bottle, carefully levelling each scoop
of powder with the flat blade of a knife
and adding the exact amount of boiled
water.

"Good girl. We'll make up his bottles
every morning and keep them in
the fridge so that when he's hungry
we've got one ready. We'll also have to
find some eucalyptus leaves and start
introducing him to those. At first he'll get
most of his nutrition from the milk but at

his age he'd be starting to eat leaves if he was in the wild."

They decided to make the dining room into a koala room. Dad cleared out the table and chairs apart from one comfy armchair and covered the carpet with an old rug so it didn't matter if he pooped on it. "We'll need to build him an indoor climbing centre out of wood," said Mum. "Joeys love to climb. However, that can wait for another day."

They put his basket in one corner and for the rest of the day, Ruby lay on the rug with Cooper, watching it, refusing to leave at all. Mum brought her lunch in so she could keep guard. Pablo was

exhausted from everything that had happened and didn't wake up until the evening. Ruby heard a snuffling and then saw his dark nose sticking out of the basket. His mouth opened and a plaintive little mew came out.

"Mum! Pablo's awake and he's crying!" said Ruby, running into the kitchen where Mum was chatting to Dad as he cooked supper.

"OK, you can heat up a bottle like I showed you in the bottle warmer," said Mum.

Ruby hurried about the kitchen. As soon as the bottle was warm enough, she took it through to Mum, who was sitting on a chair, cuddling Pablo. He was clinging on to her arms, making distressed cries.

Ruby handed Mum the bottle and knelt on the floor beside her knees as Mum touched Pablo's mouth with the teat. He moved his head away and continued crying.

The sound seemed to cut through Ruby. "Mum, he's really upset."

"He's hungry and confused," said Mum. She tried again but the joey wouldn't open his mouth.

"I'll go and get a pipette from the kitchen – I can use it to drop milk into his mouth and we can try teaching him to feed from a bottle another time," said Mum. "Can you hold him? I'll only be a few minutes."

Ruby nodded and swapped places with Mum. She wrapped the blanket around Pablo, tucking him up tightly, thinking that might make him feel more like he was in his mother's pouch. Then she held him to her chest and started to walk slowly round the room. In the wild, he would have swayed gently on his mother's back as she climbed through the trees. Maybe he missed that movement and it would help him to settle. Her plan worked; Pablo's cries quietened. Picking up the bottle, Ruby held it upside down until a drop formed on the end of the teat. She held it close to Pablo's mouth. His nose twitched and his pink tongue came out. He tasted the milk and then opened his mouth. Ruby slipped the teat inside. She'd fed baby animals at the sanctuary before and she made sure to hold Pablo fairly upright so he could swallow the milk without choking. He started to suck, tentatively at first as he got used to the bottle and teat, but as he swallowed the milk she felt him start to suck more strongly. "Good boy, that's it," she encouraged softly. "I know it's a change but you need to drink."

Pablo settled in her arms, sucking rhythmically at the bottle. Ruby felt a wave of happiness as she cradled him.

She heard a soft laugh. Her eyes flicked to the door. Her mum was standing there, smiling. "Tara's right. You really are a natural," she said warmly.

Ruby felt a rush of pride. "I said I'd be a good caretaker."

"You did," her mum said. She came over and this time, she was the one who knelt on the floor as Ruby continued to feed Pablo. "Now he knows what a bottle is, we'll hopefully find him much easier to feed."

When Pablo was finished with his bottle, Mum checked her watch. "He'll sleep for a few hours now before he wakes up for the night. Why don't you tuck him back into his basket and we'll have supper."

Ruby did as her mum said. She looked at the little koala curled up by himself in the basket. He looked lonely. It must be hard for him without his mum to cuddle.

Maybe that was why he had started crying when he woke up. She thought for a moment then hurried upstairs.

"Where are you going?" Dad called. "Supper's almost on the table."

"I'm getting something for Pablo!" Ruby went to her room and found a cuddly toy koala. She took it downstairs and tucked it into the basket next to Pablo. In his sleep, he snuggled closer to it. Ruby smiled happily and left him to sleep.

Mum stayed up with Pablo that night, feeding him every few hours when he

was hungry and keeping him company
as he explored the dining room. Ruby set
her alarm clock for 5am and took over
then so Mum could go to bed.

Later in the morning, Pablo was sleeping happily in his basket. Mum came back downstairs and yawned. "I'm going to have to try and have a nap each day while he's needing quite so many feeds at night," she said.

"We need to make him an indoor climbing frame," said Ruby eagerly. While Mum had been sleeping she had been researching how to care for orphaned koalas on the internet. "And get him some eucalyptus leaves. A nine-month-old koala needs to eat approximately 150g of leaves a day. I could take Cooper out and find some?"

"Good plan," said Mum. "You do that

and I'll go and have a lie down. Do you want Dad to come with you?"

"No, I'll be fine with Cooper," said Ruby. Taking scissors to cut the leaves and a bag to carry them in, she set off. She knew exactly where she was going. There was a small bush reserve with gum trees at the end of the street.

As she and Cooper approached the bush reserve, a girl's voice called, "Hi!"

Ruby jumped and spun round, dropping the scissors. A girl around her age was coming out of the last house on the street, which had been empty for several months. She was wearing shorts and had brown hair, freckles and small dark eyes that had a friendly look. Cooper trotted over to say hello.

"What are you doing here?" said Ruby.

"Um." The girl looked a bit surprised as she patted Cooper. "Well, I live here."

"You can't," said Ruby, frowning. "That house is empty."

"It was, but we moved in two days ago," said the girl. "What are you doing here?"

"Picking eucalyptus leaves," said Ruby. "Your eyes look like a koala's." She saw the girl look surprised. "Was that rude?" she said quickly. "I didn't mean to be."

"It wasn't rude. Koalas are cool." The

girl's smile widened. "Is this your dog?"

"Yes, he's called Cooper. He's a golden retriever and he's four years old."

"He's lovely," said the girl, fussing Cooper. "I wish I could have a dog but my mum's allergic. I'm Kirra, by the way. What's your name?"

"Ruby Amanda Turner," said Ruby. "I live at number 231 Bateman Street with my mum, Lisa, and my dad, Brad."

"We're neighbours then," said the girl, looking pleased.

Ruby studied her for a moment and then decided she liked this new girl with koala eyes. Remembering her manners, she wiped her hand on her shorts and

held it out.
"Pleased to
meet you,
Kirra."

Kirra's
eyes
twinkled
as she stepped
forward and shook it.

"And I'm pleased to meet you too, Ruby
Amanda Turner."

There was a pause. Ruby wondered
what to say. It was easy with animals,
but what did you do with people?

Thankfully, Kirra broke the silence.
"So, why are you collecting eucalyptus

leaves?" She picked up the scissors as she spoke and gave them to Ruby, holding the closed blades in her hand as she passed them over.

"I'm a koala caretaker and the joey I'm looking after needs some leaves," said Ruby.

"Really?" breathed Kirra. "That's so cool. What's he or she called?"

Ruby told Kirra all about Pablo and Kirra helped her pick some eucalyptus leaves. As they chatted, Ruby found out that Kirra loved drawing and painting as much as she did. Then Kirra told Ruby how she'd been nervous about moving to a new house. They realised they were both going to be starting at the same school in January. "We'll be able to hang round together!" said Kirra in delight.

Ruby checked her watch. "I need to go home now," she said. "Mum told me to be back by twelve and it's ten minutes to noon."

"Look, any time you want to pick leaves for Pablo just call in. I'd . . ." Kirra gave Ruby a hopeful look. "I'd really like to see him one day?"

Ruby wondered why the other girl's voice had gone up at the end, as if she was asking a question. Of course she would like to see Pablo. Anyone would. "OK. Goodbye," she said.

Kirra's face fell. Ruby wasn't very good at reading people's expressions but she thought Kirra looked disappointed.

"I like Kirra," Ruby told Cooper as she walked home with him. "You liked her too, didn't you?" He wagged his tail. Ruby smiled and skipped a few steps. She didn't know why but she suddenly felt all light and happy.

Chapter Six

Pablo woke up earlier that evening. Ruby was still awake when she heard Mum getting his bottle ready. She always found it hard to sleep but now, with Pablo downstairs, it was harder than ever! She went into the koala room.

"Ruby, you should be in bed," Mum

said. But Ruby's eyes were fixed on Pablo as he emerged from his blankets.

"I'm not tired," she told Mum. "I'll stay up with him."

"Not all night you won't," said Mum. "But you can stay up for a while. Why don't you amuse him why I warm up his bottle?"

Pablo's paws scrabbled at the edge of the basket, then he heaved himself over the edge and landed with a soft thump on the rug. Looking around slowly, he fixed his eyes on the comfy chair and started padding towards it. "Where are you going?" Ruby said to him. Pablo reached the chair and, standing up on

his back legs, dug
his claws into the
fabric. He started
to climb up it.
"It's not a tree!"
Ruby said, but he

looked so happy climbing
that she let him. He reached the back of
the chair and walked along it as if it was
a tree branch.

"That joey definitely needs a climbing
frame," said Mum, as she came in with
his bottle. She scooped him up. "We'd
better go to the garden centre to buy
some wood and rope and also to the
shopping centre to get a baby gate.

Then we can leave him to climb without worrying that he'll escape into the rest of the house and get into trouble." She placed Pablo gently into Ruby's arms. "What do you think? Should we go tomorrow?"

Ruby didn't want to go to the shopping centre but if Pablo needed her to . . . As she felt the soft warm weight of him and looked down into his dark eyes, Ruby made up her mind. "OK. We can go tomorrow."

After he had drunk his milk, Pablo set off round the room again, exploring every corner. Ruby fetched the leaves she had picked earlier. She'd been careful to pick delicate young leaves that would be softer on his mouth but Pablo only seemed to want to eat the stalks. He spat the soft bits out and chewed the tough stalks.

Ruby grinned. Pablo was fussy about food, just like her. "You just have the bits you like," she told him. "That's OK by me." She yawned.

"Bedtime," said Mum.

Ruby gave Pablo and Cooper each a hug and went to the door.

"Night, Rubes," Mum called after her as she went upstairs.

As soon as Ruby stepped into the air-conditioned shopping centre the next morning, she knew that agreeing to come had been a mistake. The lights were so bright, Christmas music was playing loudly and there were people everywhere. They bustled past her, their shopping bags knocking against Ruby, their voices loud as they talked into mobile phones and chattered to each other. Ruby shrank closer to her mum's side.

"We're doing this for Pablo," her mum said softly. "You can do this, Ruby."

Thinking about Pablo made Ruby feel a little better. She recited koala facts in

her head as she and Mum made their way to the baby store. A little boy was crouching down on the floor, playing with a toy fire engine. Its lights flashed and it made a loud siren sound as he pushed it around. The knot of tension in Ruby's tummy tightened.

Mum pointed to a display of super-soft cushions. "Why don't we get one of those for Pablo?"

Ruby hurried over to them, away from the noisy fire engine.

She chose a cushion with flowers on and Mum picked up a stair gate. Ruby was glad to see that they didn't need to queue at the till. The sooner they bought the gate and cushion, the sooner they could get back into the quiet of their car.

They were just on their way out when a lady came up to them. Ruby realised it was Maureen, one of the volunteers at the sanctuary. "Getting ready for the new arrival," she said with a nod to the stairgate.

"He's not a new arrival," Ruby said. "We've had him two days now."

Maureen looked puzzled. She turned to Mum. "He? So you know it's a boy then?"

It was Ruby's turn to feel puzzled. What was Maureen talking about? Of course they knew Pablo was a boy!

"We've got to dash!" Mum said to Maureen. "Sorry, catch up soon!"

She walked briskly out of the shop. Ruby had to jog to keep up. "What did Maureen mean?" she asked her mum. "Why did she ask if we know Pablo's a boy?"

Mum stopped and looked down at Ruby. An expression that Ruby couldn't identify fleeted across her mum's face. She sighed. "OK, Ruby, I've got something to tell you. I'm pregnant."

Ruby's frown deepened. "Pregnant? You mean you're going to have a baby?"

"Yes, in four months' time. It'll be a little brother or sister for you."

Ruby started to shake her head. "But I don't want a brother or sister." Her voice rose. "I don't want you to have a baby!" Babies cried and made a mess. A baby would change everything.

"Ruby, try to calm down," said Mum gently. But Ruby couldn't calm down. The lights were too bright. The music and voices were too loud. The smell of frying onions from a nearby hot dog stand was making her feel sick and her skin seemed to be getting tighter and tighter. A baby wailed in a buggy as his mum wheeled it past. The noise stabbed through her. She could feel herself losing control. She didn't want to but she couldn't help it. A shout burst out of her.

"No!" Ruby crouched on the floor of the shopping centre, curling her arms around her body protectively. "No! No! No!"

"Ruby." Her mum dropped the stair gate and crouched beside her. She put her hands on Ruby's arms and talked in a low soothing voice. "Come on now. You're going to be OK. Let's get you home. Pablo needs feeding."

Pablo. Ruby managed to make her legs work and stood up. Still feeling like she was screaming inside, she followed her mum to the car park. Once they were in the quiet of the car, they sat there, neither of them speaking.

"I'm sorry," Mum said softly. "Dad and I have been trying to find the right moment to tell you. We wanted to wait until we knew everything was OK."

"With the baby?" said Ruby.

Her mum nodded.

"And is it?" Ruby asked.

"Yes."

"So, it's not like me. It's not autistic," said Ruby. "It's . . ." Her tummy swirled and she felt very odd. *"Normal."*

"Ruby, no one can tell if a child is going to be autistic until they're born and start growing up," said Mum. "But autistic or not, it doesn't matter one bit.

Dad and I will love the baby, just like we love you." She reached over and gently took hold of Ruby's chin, turning her face so she could look into her eyes. "Ruby. Dad and I wouldn't change you for the world. We love you exactly the way you are and we won't love you any the less just because we have a new baby. There'll just be more love to go around."

Ruby didn't say anything. How could that be true? If you had a certain amount of milk in a bottle and you gave half to one joey and half to another, they wouldn't get as much as if they'd had the whole bottle to themselves. "Things don't work like that," she pointed out, pulling back from Mum's hand.

"Love does," said Mum. She thought for a moment. "Look at it this way. Do you love Cooper any the less just because you now have Pablo to love too?"

Ruby's frown deepened. Mum was right. Although she had Pablo to love now, she still had just as much love for

Cooper. "No," she said slowly. "I love Cooper just the same."

"There you go then." Mum kissed her finger and then gently touched the very end of Ruby's nose with a quick, feather-light touch. It was the way she had kissed her when Ruby was little and hadn't even liked Mum or Dad touching her. "And I'll always love you just the same. Nothing and no one can ever change that. Not a new baby. Not anything."

Ruby nodded and felt the tight knot inside her start to loosen slightly.

Mum started the engine and then drove them home.

Chapter Seven

"This is looking good, but we could do with some big eucalyptus branches too so he can learn how to pull the leaves off himself," said Dad as he and Ruby finished building Pablo's indoor climbing frame that afternoon.

"I could go and get some from outside

Kirra's house," suggested Ruby.

"Are you sure that's OK?" said Dad.

Ruby nodded. Of course it was. Kirra had said she could come back any time. "Yes. I'll take Cooper. Kirra likes him."

She set off with a pair of secateurs. It was a hot day, the sun beating down out of a cloudless sky. When Ruby got to Kirra's house she opened the gate and went inside the garden.

"Hey there!" Kirra got up from where she had been lying in the grass under the shade of a tree. Cooper bounded over and she stroked his ears.

Ruby felt a strange lifting feeling in her chest as Kirra jogged over. "Hi," she said, realising her mouth was pulling up into a smile.

"I was hoping you'd come again. It's kind of lonely not knowing anyone here," said Kirra.

"I need branches." Ruby explained about the indoor climbing frame.

"I'll help you get some," said Kirra and they worked together, choosing suitable branches and cutting them down with Ruby's dad's secateurs. An extra branch fell and Cooper picked it up in his mouth and trotted round the garden, his tail waving.

"He's such an awesome dog. You're so lucky," said Kirra.

Ruby smiled. She wasn't used to other kids telling her she was lucky. Most of the time they just said she was weird.

"Do you want to stay for tea?" asked Kirra. "I'm sure my mum won't mind."

Ruby bit her lip. Did she want to stay? It was Tuesday. That meant dinner should be roast chicken and mashed potato. Kirra's family might not know that. But she liked Kirra and she did want to stay and talk to her some more. "Um, what will we eat? I don't like some food."

Kirra smiled. "Don't worry. My little

sister's really fussy about food. Mum won't mind if there's stuff you don't want to eat."

It sounded OK. "I'll have to ask my mum and dad," Ruby said.

She hurried home with Cooper.

"That's lovely of her to invite you round," said Mum when Ruby told her what Kirra had asked. "Of course you can go."

"What if I don't like the food?" said Ruby doubtfully.

"Just try to eat what they have and if you really can't then just be polite and say thank you but you're not hungry," said Mum.

Ruby nodded. That sounded OK. "Can I take Cooper?"

"If Kirra's mum's allergic to dogs then probably not," said Mum. "But you can always ask Kirra here another time."

It felt strange walking round to Kirra's house without Cooper but she told herself it would be fine. She could see Cooper as soon as she got home and she did like Kirra and wanted to see her again.

To her relief, dinner wasn't too bad. The mashed potato didn't have lumps. It was really smooth. There were also peas, which Ruby liked, and she was allowed to help herself so she was able to make sure they didn't touch her potato. "No thank you," she said politely when Kirra's mum offered her some pork in gravy. "I just like potato and peas."

Kirra's mum smiled. "That's fine, honey. You have what you want. There's fruit and ice cream for dessert so you can fill up on that."

Kirra's little sister, Izzy, watched Ruby curiously. She was two. She didn't want the pork either and she didn't say much apart from "no".

"Do you love your little sister?" Ruby asked Kirra when they left the table.

Kirra looked surprised. "Um . . . yes. Why do you ask?"

Ruby stared at the floor. "My parents are having a baby."

Kirra gave her a sympathetic look. "Oh. Do you feel a bit freaked about it? I felt a bit weird when Mum and Dad had Izzy but it'll be fine. You'll see. So how's Pablo? What's he doing? Does he like the leaves?"

Ruby felt a rush of relief as she turned to her favourite topic of conversation – Pablo. She answered all of Kirra's questions and told her everything the little joey had been doing. "He likes his new climbing frame," she said happily. "We let him try it out just before I came here. He wasn't really properly awake but I reckon he'll go on it more this evening."

"Can I come round to your house?" The words burst out of Kirra as if she'd been holding them in.

Ruby blinked. "Yes. Yes, you can."

Kirra beamed and Ruby felt her mouth turn up into a matching smile.

"When?" said Kirra eagerly.

Ruby frowned. "Pablo sleeps in the day. He's nocturnal, which means he's awake at night."

Kirra grinned. "Then I guess we'd better have a sleepover!"

Ruby blinked again. She'd never even had a friend round, let alone have one sleep over. There was a special bed that could pull out from under her own bed but it had never been used. She thought how nice it would be to have Kirra there to meet Pablo.

"OK," she decided. "I'll ask if we can have a sleepover on Friday night."

"Cool," said Kirra. "I'll check with Mum but I'm sure she'll say yes. Now, should we do some drawing before you go?"

For the next hour the two girls drew and painted. When it was time for Kirra's mum to walk Ruby home, Kirra handed her a picture. It was of a koala and next to it was a girl with chin-length dark hair and brown eyes. Kira had written underneath with a special gel pen the words: "My friend Ruby."

"Here," she said, handing it to Ruby and looking at the ground shyly.

Ruby read the words and felt the same feeling she got when Pablo looked at her with his little dark eyes – her heart seemed to swell like a balloon was being blown up inside it.

"Do you like it?" said Kirra.

Ruby smiled. "Yes," she told her. "I do."

Chapter Eight

Ruby cuddled Pablo. His claws were
bunched in her dressing gown, his velvet-
soft head nestled under her chin. She
could feel the soft weight of him in her
arms. It was five-thirty in the morning
and the end of his awake time. He
yawned sleepily. She walked round the

room, knowing he liked the movement. It was her favourite time of the day, when it was just her and Pablo in the peace of the early morning.

"Tonight you'll meet Kirra," she whispered to him. "She's going to stay here. I've never had anyone sleep in my room before." She kissed his head. Two new things were going to happen that day – Kirra was coming to stay that evening and in the afternoon, Ruby was going with her mum and dad for a baby scan.

Mum had shown Ruby a video on YouTube so Ruby knew it was a way of seeing if the baby was OK. Ruby wanted to see the scan, it looked interesting, but she wasn't sure about going into hospital, with lots of people, bright lights and bad smells. She wished they could take Cooper. She knew she'd like it more if he was there but when she'd asked Mum, she had said dogs weren't allowed.

Ruby snuggled Pablo down in his basket, tucking the blankets around him and making sure he had his toy koala. He dug his claws into its back and made a happy snuffling, squeaking noise. Ruby smiled and, leaving him to sleep, she started cleaning the bottles.

At the hospital, Mum had to lie on a bed. Ruby felt a shiver of horror as the sonographer – the person doing the scan – squeezed a big lump of gooey clear gel on to Mum's bare tummy. She backed as far away as possible, feeling sick. However, looking at the grainy image on the screen was interesting and the sonographer told them it was a baby boy. Ruby started to ask lots of questions: how long was the baby, how much did the baby weigh, what did it eat, and when would it be born?

Michelle, the sonographer, answered all of Ruby's questions. Ruby liked her; she explained things clearly and sensibly.

Ruby was quiet on the way back to the car.

"Well, what did you think?" said Dad.

"Scans are interesting," said Ruby. "Can I see a pregnant animal being scanned one day?"

"I can try and arrange it at the sanctuary," said Mum. "But what did you think about the baby?"

Ruby shrugged. Mum and Dad seemed to be waiting for her to say something. "It's got a big head," she said. "It's going to look weird." A more interesting thought crossed her mind. "If you scan an animal, how do you get them to lie still? And do they mind having that jelly stuff on their tummy? What if they try and lick it off? And what about their fur? Does that stop the scan working?"

Mum sighed and started to answer her questions until Ruby ran out of things to ask.

"So, Ruby, we're going to start turning the spare room into a nursery," said Dad. "We'll need to decorate it. Do you fancy helping paint it? We can get out the rollers and big brushes and wall paint."

Ruby thought about how messy it would be. Wall paint was thick and gloopy. Blobs would fall off the wall and maybe on to her skin. She shuddered and shook her head. Getting ready for

the baby wasn't her job; it was Mum
and Dad's. Just like looking after the
baby wouldn't be her job. It would be
Mum and Dad's. She didn't know what
to do with babies. Anxiety curled in
her tummy at the thought of the baby
coming to live in their house with them.
She didn't like things that were unknown
and unfamiliar. "I don't want to help,"
she said firmly.

This time both Mum and Dad sighed.

Kirra arrived at five o'clock with a
sleepover bag and four large branches of
eucalyptus leaves. "I thought you could

do with some more of these," Kirra said, thrusting the branches into Ruby's hands with a grin.

"Thanks!" said Ruby happily.

"Looks like you've been painting," Kirra's dad said, nodding at Dad's paint-spattered jeans.

"Yes, getting a nursery ready for the new arrival," said Dad, smiling at Mum. "Kirra, Ruby tells me you like painting too," he went on. "Maybe you girls would like to give me a hand later? The walls are done now but it's looking kind of plain."

Kirra started to nod eagerly but Ruby broke in. "Kirra's here to see Pablo," she told Dad. "Not to paint a room for your baby." She turned to Kirra. "Take your shoes off and come wash your hands."

The girls left Kirra's bag on the stairs and went into the dining room. "Oh, wow!" breathed Kirra as she saw the big indoor climbing frame.

"We can tie the branches on to it. It helps him get used to pulling the leaves off just like he'll have to when he goes back to the wild," said Ruby.

"Where is he?" asked Kirra.

"Asleep," said Ruby. "He just had a feed so he won't wake up now until about nine. Come and see." She beckoned Kirra over to the basket and they crouched down together, their heads almost touching. Ruby very gently separated the blankets so that Kirra could see the baby koala snoozing, cuddled up to his toy.

"Oh," breathed Kirra, looking almost lost for words. "He's so cute."

Ruby smiled proudly. It was really nice to show Pablo to someone and Kirra was sensible – she was keeping her voice quiet and soft. Ruby felt very glad she'd invited her round. She'd been a bit worried because she'd read that koala caretakers shouldn't let the joeys they were looking after be handled by too many people in case they caught germs.

But Mum had said it would be fine if it was just Kirra. "He'll wake up later and you can help feed him," Ruby said.

Kirra beamed.

At nine o'clock, Pablo woke up and crawled out of his basket, making hungry mewing sounds. "That means he wants his milk," Ruby told Kirra. She showed Kirra how to hold him and how to tip the bottle into his mouth, always making sure the teat was full of milk so that no air bubbles got in because they would give him a sore tummy.

Kirra loved feeding him. "It's just like holding a baby," she said. She smiled at Ruby. "You'll be a total expert by the time your mum has her baby."

Ruby frowned. "I won't look after the baby. Mum and Dad will."

Kirra looked surprised. "I know, but he'll be your brother. Don't you want to help? I liked helping with Izzy when she was little. There was loads to do and—"

"I think Pablo's had enough now. He wants to get down and play," Ruby interrupted. She didn't want to talk about the baby. Her chest was tightening at the thought. *No*, she thought quickly, breathing out through her nose and trying to calm herself down. *I'm not going to get upset in front of Kirra.* She took Pablo off Kirra. "Look how well he can climb!"

Pablo stood up on his back legs, his claws digging into the wood. He pulled himself up the vertical branches and then crawled across the top, making excited squeaking noises as he spotted the eucalyptus they had tied on. He headed towards it. At one point he lost his balance and swung to one side. Kirra gasped in alarm but Ruby just smiled as he used another branch to straighten himself and then pulled himself upright again. He reached the eucalyptus and settled in a fork in the climbing frame to pull off the leaves. Chewing the stalks, he stared at the girls. Opening his mouth, he squeaked at them again.

"He is just the cutest thing," said Kirra. "Thank you for letting me come and see him."

They played with Pablo until Mum said it was time to go to sleep. They settled down in their beds – Kirra sleeping on the pull-out bed. She'd brought three cuddly toy animals with her – a tiger, a platypus and a rabbit. They talked about animals as they lay in bed. Ruby told Kirra lots of animals facts. She heard Kirra's breathing start to get slow and regular just like Pablo's did when he was falling asleep.

"OK, girls, time to stop talking," said Mum, putting her head round the door.

"Kirra, Ruby will be up early in the morning but it's fine if you want to stay in bed."

"Thanks, Mrs Turner," Kirra said sleepily and then she turned over and fell asleep.

Ruby stayed awake a bit longer. It was strange having someone in her bedroom with her. Different. *Do I like it?* she wondered. She decided that she did.

That's because Kirra's my friend, Ruby thought and, with a smile, she closed her eyes.

Chapter Nine

Ruby woke up in the early morning
just as she always did. Leaving Kirra
to sleep, she crept out of the bedroom
and went downstairs. Mum had fallen
asleep in the chair and Pablo was curled
up in his basket with his toy. That was
strange. He was usually moving round

and looking for a final feed. Feeling disappointed that she wouldn't get to give him a feed, Ruby collected the used bottles and set about sterilising them and making up new feeds. Mum had put the dirty blankets beside the washing machine. Ruby put the washing on and then put the breakfast things out – bowls, plates, glasses, cutlery, along with cereals and orange juice. She liked setting the table, making sure that the cutlery was perfectly lined up beside the bowls and plates.

At six-thirty, her mum came through to the kitchen, her hair rumpled from sleeping in the chair. "I'm going upstairs to sleep some more," she said, yawning.

"When can I wake Kirra up?" Ruby asked.

"Leave it until seven-thirty," said Mum.

Ruby sighed impatiently. She hated waiting for things. Luckily she didn't have to wait long as Kirra woke up at seven and came to find her. Dad got up too and they all had breakfast together. After breakfast, the girls sat at the table and drew pictures of the animals in Ruby's encyclopaedia.

"You'd better get your things together, Kirra," Dad said at nine-thirty. "Your dad said he'd be here to pick you up around ten."

"Can I see Pablo once more before I go?" Kirra asked Ruby.

"He'll be asleep but you can look at him," said Ruby.

They washed their hands and went into the koala room. To Ruby's surprise, Pablo had crawled out of his basket and was curled up on the rug. That wasn't normal. Pablo usually slept in his basket until lunchtime when he had a quick feed and went back to sleep again.

"He's so sweet," Kirra sighed, kneeling beside the sleeping joey.

But Ruby's skin was prickling. Why was Pablo out of his basket? He whimpered slightly in his sleep. She

picked him up. He usually stirred in his sleep when she did that and cuddled closer but now he just felt floppy. He blinked as she moved him and Ruby saw that his eyes looked dull. "Kirra! Get my dad," she said in alarm. "I think Pablo's ill!"

Dad had a quick look at Pablo and then went to wake Mum. She came downstairs in her dressing gown and took Pablo off Ruby.

"You're right, Ruby, he doesn't look

very well," Mum said, examining him. She gently pulled down Pablo's eyelids to check his eyes, looked in his mouth and used a stethoscope to listen to his breathing. She offered him one of the bottles Ruby had made up that morning but he wouldn't open his mouth. Ruby and Kirra watched anxiously.

"What's the matter with him, Mum?" Ruby asked, fighting to keep her voice soft.

"I think he may have an infection. I'd better take him to the sanctuary so that one of the vets can look at him," said Mum.

"Can I come?" Ruby asked.

"No, you stay here with Dad," said Mum.

Ruby started to argue but Mum was firm. Ruby could feel herself starting to get more and more upset. She was Pablo's caretaker; she needed to be with him.

"Ruby, you need to stay calm," Dad told her gently. "This isn't helping Pablo. Mum should be getting him to the sanctuary not arguing with you."

Ruby breathed out deeply. Dad was right. The sooner Pablo got to the vet, the better. Mum had put him in his basket and he was curled up next to his teddy, breathing with raspy breaths.

"Poor little Pablo," said Kirra as they walked with Mum to the car.

"Don't worry, girls," Mum said as she carried the basket to the car. "He's going to be fine."

"You don't know that," said Ruby, clenching and unclenching her fists as she tried to fight the anxiety that was spiralling inside her. How had this happened? Why had Pablo got sick?

"He will be. Koala joeys often get infections," said Mum. "Antibiotics usually sort things out."

"Usually's not definitely," said Ruby unhappily.

Mum drove away.

As she did so, another car drew up. It was Kirra's dad.

"Is everything OK?" he said, looking at their faces.

"The koala joey's not too well so Lisa has just run him into the sanctuary," Dad explained. "We think he might have an infection. The symptoms came on quickly."

"He was fine yesterday," said Kirra. "He played with me and Ruby and we cuddled him and fed him."

Ruby stared. Suddenly everything made sense. "You!" she said, pointing at Kirra. "It was your fault!"

"Me?" squeaked Kirra.

Ruby's voice rose. "Yes! Pablo was fine until you came. You must have brought germs with you yesterday!"

"Ruby!" Dad said sharply as Kirra's face crumpled. "That will do. Pablo's illness has nothing to do with Kirra, nothing at all."

Everything was too much for Ruby. Feeling overwhelmed, she turned and ran to her room. Seeing Cooper, she flung herself down beside him, sobs tearing out of her. She should never have let Kirra hold him. What if Pablo was really ill? What if he died?

She heard her dad apologising to Kirra and her dad. "I'm so sorry about that.

Ruby is really upset about Pablo but that's no excuse. I'll have words with her when she's calmed down. Pablo being sick really has nothing to do with you, Kirra. I promise."

Ruby kept sobbing into Cooper's warm solid neck. She heard her dad say goodbye and then she heard his footsteps coming into her bedroom.

"Ruby?"

Her sobs were calming now but she refused to look round.

Her dad crouched down beside her. "Ruby, listen to me. Pablo being sick is not Kirra's fault. For a start, she washed her hands and took off her shoes just like we all do, but also infections take several days to develop before a joey shows signs of being sick. Kirra was here yesterday. The infection Pablo has at the moment has nothing to do with her."

Ruby sniffed. She could feel the salty tracks of tears on her cheeks.

"You really upset her, Ruby," Dad went on. "People don't do that to their friends. You're going to have to say sorry."

Cooper licked Ruby's neck. She kept stroking him, still refusing to look round or speak.

Just then, Dad's phone rang. "It's your mum." Now, Ruby did look round.

"Oh that's good news, love," Dad said after a pause, sounding relieved. "Great. So just antibiotics and some TLC? You'll be home soon? Great – yes, I'll tell Ruby. Drive safely."

"Pablo?" Ruby gasped, her eyes wide. "Is he going to be OK?"

Her dad nodded. "He's got a mild infection. The vet's given him a shot of antibiotics and your mum has some more medicine to give him at home. He's going to be fine."

The breath rushed out of Ruby. "Oh." She swallowed. "That's good."

"Very good." Dad hesitated as if he was going to say something more but

then he gave a small shake of his head.
"Go and wash your face and hands.
Mum will be back soon."

Ruby stayed with Pablo all day,
cuddling him and persuading him to
have little drinks of milk. She didn't go
to bed until midnight. When she finally
went upstairs, she lay with her eyes open.
She should be tired but she just wasn't
sleepy. Now she knew Pablo was going
to be OK she kept thinking about Kirra.
She remembered the way Kirra's face
had crumpled and tears had sprung
to her eyes when she had shouted at

her that morning and it made her feel
uncomfortable inside. Trying not to think
about it, she recited koala facts until she
finally fell asleep.

Despite her late night, she woke early.
Mum had fallen asleep in the chair
again, an empty bottle of milk in her
hand. Pablo was walking slowly around
the base of the climbing frame. He
wasn't quite as lively as he usually was
but he looked a lot better than he did the
day before. Seeing Ruby, he squeaked.

"I'll get you some more milk," she said.
She fetched a fresh bottle and then sat on

the floor with him, leaning against the chair where Mum was sleeping. When Pablo finished his milk, she cuddled him until his eyes started to close. Feeling a soft touch on her shoulder, she looked round and saw that Mum had woken up. She was smiling sleepily down at Ruby, her free hand resting on her rounded tummy.

"You know, Ruby, you're going to be a wonderful big sister," she said softly.

Ruby frowned. "But how will I know what to do?

I've never been a sister before."

"Well, it's just like looking after a joey to start with," said Mum. "Human babies need feeding – you need to measure out their milk and sterilise their bottles. You also have to keep them clean and play with them. Your baby brother will need all the things Pablo does."

Ruby thought about it. If it was just like looking a joey then maybe it wouldn't be too bad. "I am good at being a koala caretaker, aren't I?"

"The best," said Mum.

"So, maybe I will be a good baby caretaker too," said Ruby thoughtfully. She saw that her Mum's eyes looked shiny. "Are you going to cry?" said Ruby curiously. "Have I made you sad?"

"No." Mum shook her head. "You've made me happy, sweetie."

Ruby felt confused. She tried her hardest but she just didn't understand people.

She cuddled Pablo and thought some more about the baby. A thought struck her. She'd helped get the dining room ready for Pablo because she was his caretaker. If she was going to be a good baby caretaker, then maybe she should help get the baby's room ready as well. But how? She hadn't helped paint the walls but maybe there was something she could do . . .

Chapter Ten

"Hi." Ruby stood on the step of Kirra's house. Kirra had opened the door when she knocked and now she was standing there, looking at Ruby warily. The expression on her face reminded Ruby of the look injured animals had when they were brought into the sanctuary.

"Hi," Kirra said, swallowing.

"Pablo's getting better!" said Ruby.

"That's good," muttered Kirra.

"It is, isn't it?" said Ruby. She felt puzzled that Kira didn't seem happier. "You can come and see him. Your germs didn't make him ill."

She waited for Kirra to say something but Kirra just looked at the floor.

"I need you to come and help me with something," Ruby said, hoping that this would make Kirra speak.

"I . . . I don't think I can," said Kirra. She started to back inside the house.

"Wait." Ruby frowned at Kirra. She looked unhappy. But why? Ruby was asking her to help and telling her good news about Pablo.

Friends don't upset each other. Dad's words came back to her.

Maybe Kirra was still upset because of the day before? Ruby bit her lip. She knew what she should do if she upset someone but she hated it.

"No. Don't. I . . . I . . . I'm sorry!" Ruby burst out.

The words hung in the air. Kirra looked startled.

"I really am sorry," Ruby repeated, realising she meant it. She was sorry that she had made Kirra look so unhappy. "Will you be my friend again? Please?"

Kirra's mouth turned upwards.

"Are you happy now?" Ruby asked hopefully.

"Yes." Kirra's smile got wider. "I am. I do want to be your friend, Ruby. It was horrible when you blamed me for Pablo being ill. Your mum rang and told me

that it wasn't really my fault and that you were sorry but that you're not very good at saying sorry."

"I'm not," Ruby admitted honestly. "I really don't like saying sorry at all. It makes me feel funny inside."

"But you still did it," said Kirra, opening the door properly. "So we're friends again."

Ruby felt a rush of warmth. Now she felt happy too.

"What do you need me to help you with?" Kirra asked.

Ruby grinned. "Come to my house and I'll show you!"

The two of them knelt by the walls in the new nursery. Ruby was drawing a design on the pale blue walls in pencil – a mural of lots of different kinds of wild animals copied from her animal encyclopaedia – and Kirra, who didn't mind using thick gloopy paint, was filling the design in with careful strokes. On the walk to Ruby's house, Ruby had explained her plan.

"Dad's painted the spare room but it looks very plain. A baby's nursery should have interesting things for the baby to look at, just like Pablo needs things to climb on. Will you help me?"

"Of course!" Kirra had said. "What

things are we going to paint?"

Ruby had grinned. "Lots of animals, of course!"

The two of them made a very good team. Ruby was a faster drawer than Kirra – she only needed to draw a few carefully placed lines to create the animals' shapes – and Kirra loved adding the paint.

"It looks really beautiful," said Kirra, as she sat back on her heels and admired the parts of the mural they had already completed.

"It does," said Ruby. "It's very different to how it was before."

"Do you mind that?" Kirra asked her.

Looking round the room, Ruby realised she didn't. She liked the thought that her baby brother would grow up looking at pictures she'd drawn. She'd be able to tell him facts about all the animals on his walls.

"Hey, girls, this is looking wonderful!" said Mum, as she came in with a plate of cookies and two glasses of milk.

"Your baby had better like animals," said Kirra.

"Oh, he will," said Mum and Ruby together. Ruby smiled happily at her mum. "I'll be able to tell him about the animals and read him my animal books," she said.

"We can even get him some special
animal books just for babies that he can
touch and hold," said Mum. "Then he

won't touch yours and make them messy. I'll also get you a book on how to look after babies so you can find out what to expect."

"You're really lucky to be having a baby brother," said Kirra.

Ruby nodded and realised she was actually starting to look forward to it. Maybe having a baby added to her family wouldn't be so bad after all.

"So, here we are," said Mum, looking round at the koala enclosure. It was the final day of the summer holidays, Christmas had come and gone and it was now time for Pablo to go into the koala kindergarten with the other young koalas. He would live there for four or five months until he was old enough to be released back into the wild.

Ruby stroked Pablo. It had been wonderful being his caretaker and watching as he had grown and changed. He was a lot bigger now than when they had first found him and he felt much heavier in her arms. He ate a lot more leaves these days and didn't drink nearly as much milk. He was far more confident and was usually awake and exploring most of the night. The other evening, he had even climbed over the child gate and ended up in Ruby's bedroom! He was happy and healthy and ready to take the next step towards being released back into the wild. *And it's all because of us,* thought Ruby, feeling a rush of pleasure.

"I'll still come and visit you," she told him as he looked round with interest at his new surroundings. "But it's time for you to make friends. You're starting kindergarten and I'm starting high school. We're both going to be making friends at the same time." Ruby didn't feel the horrible clutch of panic she always used to feel when she thought about starting high school. She wasn't so worried about it now that she had Kirra to go with. They were going to travel to school together and Mum had asked if they could be in the same tutor group. They'd both bought matching pencil cases with koalas on them!

Pablo looked at her with his dark, bright eyes and Ruby felt her heart twist. She was going to miss him so much but she knew this was the right thing to do. Koalas were wild animals, not pets, and she wanted Pablo to be happy and free. She was going to be busy helping Mum and Dad look after the new baby anyway, and Mum had said that when things had settled down with the baby they could offer to be koala caretakers again for a new joey who needed a foster home.

Mum opened the door of the enclosure and Ruby stepped inside. She could see the other koalas' curious grey faces watching them from the trees. Crouching down, Ruby gently unclasped Pablo's claws and placed him on the reddy-brown ground.

He looked round at her. "Go on. Go," she said softly.

He hesitated and then very slowly started to amble towards the nearest gum tree. Ruby willed him on.

Standing on his back legs, he clasped the tree trunk and began to climb up.

Ruby's heart swelled with pride. She'd done it! She'd cared for Pablo and looked after him as best she could and now he'd be able to live the life he should. She glanced round and saw that her mum had shiny, happy tears in her eyes again. As Pablo disappeared into the branches, Ruby smiled and headed towards her mum. Pablo was going to be fine.

And so was she.

The End

Over the summer of 2019-2020, devastating bushfires blazed in Australia, causing widespread destruction. To assist those affected by the bushfires, Hachette and its employees raised funds for the Australian Red Cross and WIRES, as well making donations to the Queensland and New South Wales rural fire services. Hachette Australia also donated children's books to schools and libraries impacted by the bushfires.

Love reading about animals?
Don't miss Tilda Kelly's new book,
The Fairy Penguin!